WAR GAMES

TERRY DEARY

TWO STORIES

D1328907

WITH ILLUSTRATIONS BY
STEFANO TAMBELLINI

Barrington Stoke

For the Fallen

First published in 2004 in Great Britain by
Barrington Stoke Ltd
18 Walker Street, Edinburgh, EH3 7LP

www.barringtonstoke.co.uk

This edition first published 2013

ISBN: 978-1-78112-205-1

Printed in China by Leo

Contents

Keep off the Grass

England, June 1944

Five years after the beginning of World War 2

Chapter 1

A Seaside Town in the North

"You're going to the country, George," my mum told me.

"What for?" I asked.

She gave a sigh and wiped her hands on her apron. "Don't argue, George. That nasty Mr Hitler is dropping doodlebugs on all the big towns. We may be next. You don't want a bomb landing on your head, do you?"

"Better than going to the country," I sniffed.

"There's lots of grass in the country," Mum said.

"There's lots of grass growing in the cracks in our road. And we've got the beach nearby."

Mum sighed. "You're going, and that's it."

"Aw, Mum."

"Don't argue. I've packed your suitcase. You're leaving tomorrow."

I wandered out into the back lane and kicked at the cobble stones. My mate, Jimmy came out of his back gate and ran up to me. "I'm getting excavated tomorrow," he said.

I stared at him. "You mean sent off to the countryside," I said. "*Evacuated.*"

"Yes," he nodded. "That as well. Are you getting excavated?"

"You mean evacuated. Like I said."

"Well? Are you?" He was so excited his eyes were shining and his cheeks were as red as his hair.

"Yes," I groaned.

"It'll be good, won't it?" he asked.

I'd heard the stories about children being sent away from home because of the war. Some kids had a very bad time. They stayed in strange houses and the people that looked after them were cruel. They made them work on farms and do all the dirty jobs. I looked at Jimmy. He was so excited.

"It'll be great," I told him.

"Shall we have one last game of cricket before we go?" he asked.

"Get the bat and ball, then," I said.

The bat was a thin piece of wood we used to play with on the beach. That was before they put barbed wire up and stopped us going onto the beach. The barbed wire was there to stop the Germans landing. Why Mr Hitler would bother with a scruffy little town like ours I never knew.

The ball was a tennis ball. When you played cricket in our street, the ball would hit the cobble stones and bounce off anywhere. You had to be good to hit it. For a wicket we drew a line with some chalk on the sooty, brick wall of Mr Jackson's baker shop.

As we played other boys and girls came to join us. "Are you being evacuated?" they all asked.

"It'll be good," Jimmy told them. "George says it'll be good."

Soon we had enough people playing to make two teams of five and we started a game. I was good. That evening I was the best. I scored fifty

runs in no time and the other team was getting fed up.

Jimmy never gave up though. He bowled the ball at me so slow I'll bet it got dusty on its way to my bat. I tapped the ball gently up into the air and back to Jimmy. He caught it and held onto it, holding it up close to his body, next to his ragged, grey jumper.

"I caught it!" he shouted. "I caught it. You're out, George, I caught it. You're out."

I tried to look sad about it. "I thought you'd drop it, Jimmy," I said with a sigh.

"*You* thought I'd drop it?" he laughed. "*I* thought I'd drop it. I've never got you out before, George."

"No. Well done, Jimmy. Well done."

His eyes were shining and he looked towards the setting sun. "Tomorrow we'll be playing cricket on grass," he grinned. "Won't we, George?"

"I hope so, Jimmy," I told him.

But things never work out the way you think they will, do they?

Chapter 2
The Country

The next morning, all of us children were put on a train to the countryside. When we got off the train there was a line of frowning women on the platform. You could see their noses curl up when they looked at us.

A big man, like a teacher, made us stand in a line. The women walked up and down the line saying, "I'll have this one. Come with me, child." Their voices were as posh as the man's voice on the radio. The one who read the news.

All the pretty little girls went first, then the cute boys. Jimmy was one of the first to go. A lady in a straw hat made a big fuss over him. He waved at me as he went off happily. I knew he'd be all right.

At last there was just one kid left. Me. I was tall for my age and my hair was as tattered as my shorts and jumper. I'd had a bath just the month before but I knew I didn't smell as sweet as the ladies with their perfume.

The sun was setting and a mist began to fall. There were birds singing – not sparrows like we had back at home, in my street. These were real country birds.

The big teacher-man looked at me. "What are we going to do with you then?" he asked.

"Send me back," I muttered.

Suddenly his hand swung up and smacked me over the ear. "Don't they teach you manners where you come from?" he asked, angry as anything.

I shrugged but didn't rub my ear where it stung.

"Sir!" he hissed. "You call the gentlemen 'Sir' and the ladies 'Miss' or 'Madam'. Understand?"

I shrugged. "Suppose so."

This time his other hand came up and slammed the other side of my head. "Sir!" he growled. "You call me 'Sir'." I rocked a little. I didn't rub my ear. I didn't cry.

At that moment a woman hurried onto the platform. She had more powder and perfume than all the other women put together and her clothes had fur round the edges. She wore jewels and pearls everywhere.

"Harris!" she called to the big man who had slapped me. The man smiled a tight smile.

"Good evening, Mrs Reeve-Smith," he said and his voice was like warm grease.

"Are there any children left for me to take?" she asked. "My driver couldn't get the car started. The petrol must have been dirty. So I'm late."

The big man, Mr Harris, shook his head sadly. "All the children have been taken now," he said. "There's another lot coming here next week."

The woman looked at me standing beside Mr Harris. "What about this one?"

Mr Harris looked as if he was in pain. "Oh, dear, no! Not for you, Mrs Reeve-Smith. This one is really rough. He needs a good sorting out."

The woman gave a sigh. "I'll take him," she said. "Or else everyone in the village will have a poor child and I won't. I can't have that."

Mr Harris shook his head. "He needs sorting out."

She sniffed. "I'll send him to the grammar school with my little Rupert. They'll knock him into shape in no time."

Mr Harris shook his head. The woman looked at me properly for the first time. "Follow me, boy."

I followed her.

Chapter 3
The House

Mum was right. They had lots of grass in the country. They had so much they were cutting it and making it into hay. Horses were pulling heavy cartloads of hay back to the farms as we drove home to Mrs Reeve-Smith's house.

She never spoke. She put me in the front of the huge car beside her driver so she didn't have to sit next to me.

Her house was as large as the museum in the middle of our town. They had a stuffed lion in our museum. In the woman's house they just seemed to have stuffed people. Servants stood like dummies till Mrs Reeve-Smith reached them, then they moved sharply to open a door for her. Maids walked around like silent clockwork dolls.

My room was in the attic with the servants. It was a small room with a window that looked over miles of grass and trees. There were some farm cottages in the distance. But no rows of houses, no factories, no shops, no pubs, no noise and no children playing. "Look what you've dumped me in, Mr Hitler," I muttered.

"Who are you talking to?" a voice said from the door. A boy about the same age as me stood there. He was in a neat school uniform. "I'm Rupert Reeve-Smith." He was twice as fat as me and his eyes were as cold as his mother's.

"Hello," I said.

"You're Porter, aren't you?"

"George," I said.

"You'll be going to my school tomorrow, Porter. Mother said I had to give you my old uniform," he said. "Try it on." He held out a paper bag. I took it and then put the clothes from the bag out onto the bed. The clothes were too wide for me and too short. When I tried them on I looked like a scarecrow and smelled of washing powder.

Rupert looked at me. His eyes glinted. "The chaps at school may give you a rough time, Porter."

"Why?" I asked.

Rupert looked away. "You know ... you'll be the new boy. You look a bit odd. You talk a bit funny. They may ... make fun of you."

I shrugged. "I can look after myself. If anyone picks on me they'll feel my fist," I said softly. "They won't do it again."

Rupert looked at me sharply. "Don't even think about fighting back," he said. "If you do they'll all gang up against you. And they'll have the teachers to back them up. Just take it like a man, there's a good chap."

He turned and walked away. I looked out of the window. It was getting dark now. Stars were coming out. We never seemed to see so many stars in the town – not with the sooty air and the street lights. Not even when the blackout made the streets as dark and dangerous as a dungeon. I looked up at the sky and whispered, "When I join the army I'll come and get you for this, Mr Hitler. You'll be sorry."

I took off the baggy school clothes and climbed into the soft, white bed. As I fell off to sleep I thought about what my dad would say. His voice was whispering in my ear. "George, you are a Porter. You don't back off. You don't complain."

"No, Dad," I muttered as I fell asleep.

Chapter 4
The School

Rupert Reeve-Smith went to school in the huge Bentley car with a servant to drive him and I went with him. I was full of the biggest breakfast I'd ever had. At home we got by with a bit of dried egg and toast and a cup of tea. The Reeve-Smiths seemed to have no problem getting food.

The boys were waiting for me in the school yard. "This is Porter," Rupert said.

The neat, sneering boys closed in for the 'welcome'. First came the name-calling. "Town scum." That was one of the nice names. There were a lot of words about the smell and the dirt and how stupid people who came from towns were.

I smiled.

The boys came closer. Someone spat in my face. The spit was warm and sickly and trickled down my face. I didn't wipe it off because the boy would only spit at me again.

I smiled.

A boy grabbed my school tie and pulled it till I nearly choked. The school bell rang and those poor posh boys ran to line up at the door. I put the tie right, wiped off the spit and smiled.

After a few days they thought I was no fun. I never fought back. I never cried. I never ran

away. Like Dad said, a Porter doesn't back off.
And I never complained.

The lessons were boring, but the food was
good. Mum wrote and said she was missing me.
I wrote back and told her I was missing her –
but I was happy. Anyway there were only two
more weeks to go till the school holidays.

In those last two weeks the boring lessons
stopped and we had more sport and games on
the school field.

I ran in the races but made sure I never
won. I played football and put up with the sly
kicks and fat elbows from the other boys. I
never kicked or pushed back.

Then it came to the cricket.

The bat was full size – not the piece of wood
I played with back home. I didn't know how
anyone could miss the ball with a bat that big.

And the grass was firm and level. When the ball bounced, it bounced the same way every time – not the wild and whirling bounces of the tennis ball on the cobble stones in my back lane at home.

The game looked so easy.

Of course no one wanted me on their team. They didn't let me bat till nearly everyone was out. But, when I did bat, I stopped their jeering for a little while.

Fat Rupert was the first to bowl to me. His friends joked and he grinned as he bowled the ball at me. I swung the bat and hit the ball right back at him. He jumped so the ball passed under his feet and went speeding to the edge of the pitch. "Four runs, Rupert," someone jeered.

The smile slid off his face like jelly sliding off a plate. Next time he took a long run and threw the ball at me as hard as he could. It bounced. I swung the bat and sent the ball over the rope at the edge of the pitch without it even touching the ground again. "Six runs, Rupert," someone laughed.

Rupert was really angry. He couldn't do anything to get me out. When I'd scored fifty runs I felt sorry for him. I tapped the ball up into the air – the way I used to do for Jimmy. Rupert dropped it.

He never forgave me. The bullying started all over again and this time Rupert was leading it. It went on back at the house with slugs in my food and grass snakes in my bed. Poor snakes.

Poor, posh Rupert. Town scum were not supposed to beat boys like him at anything.

But the games teacher noticed my batting. He put me in the team for the game against the grammar school in the next village. It was the last day of term. The other school was the enemy. This game was as bitter as Mr Hitler's war.

Rupert was captain of our school team. Rupert was furious.

Chapter 5
The Game

"Porter should bat first," one of the boys told Rupert Reeve-Smith. "He's the best." It was the boy who'd spat in my face three weeks before.

Rupert turned his mean eyes on me. "Porter bats last."

The team groaned. "I'm the captain," said Rupert in a louder voice. "I decide. No one argues with me. No one." When the boys stopped talking and were silent Rupert went on, "This is a big game, chaps. Even if you lose every other game this summer, make sure you win this one. It's a war against the old enemy. Win it for the school. Win it for England." He let his eyes rest on me for a moment. "Let's show them how *gentlemen* play cricket."

The team marched out onto the pitch to play. The other school batted first. Rupert bowled badly and the enemy scored again and again.

"Come on, Reeve-Smith. Let someone else bowl," someone in our team said.

Rupert looked at him angrily and snapped, "I'm captain. I decide."

After two hours on that hot afternoon the other team had scored 152 runs. We had tea. There were sandwiches filled with beef paste and salmon, ham and cheese for us to eat. There were cream cakes and a trifle and endless bottles of lemonade. It was hard to remember there was a war on. Back home people wouldn't see that much food in a month.

But all that food seemed to send our team to sleep. They wandered back onto the pitch, batted badly and were out one after another. A tall, fair-haired boy bowled as fast as Mrs Reeve-Smith's posh car and beat our batsmen time and time again.

At last I walked out onto the pitch to bat. We had just 97 runs and needed 56 more to win. Rupert stood at the other end and looked at me with a mixture of hope and hate. "Do your best, Porter," he said.

The other team sent out their second-best bowlers to play. After all, they thought they just had to bowl out a scruffy city kid for them to win the game. But the scruffy city kid batted as if this was an easy game. It was.

When I'd scored 30 runs, they looked worried. The tall, fair-haired boy came back to bowl. He arched his back and threw the ball as fast as he could. The faster the ball came to me the faster it flew off my bat.

The crowd had gone strangely quiet now. Parents and players stood at the edge and watched the war between bat and ball. Rupert was pale and puffy faced as he played carefully at the other end of the pitch. I'd scored 50 runs while he'd only scored two.

When I reached 50 runs the crowd stirred and clapped politely. Someone shouted, "Come on, Reeve-Smith."

Mrs Reeve-Smith had appeared. "Come along, Rupert, my brave boy!" she cried. No one called to me. The people watching didn't even know my name.

The sun was low in the sky and the shadows stretched over the perfect green of the pitch.

The tall bowler went back almost to the tea tent to run up and bowl. He threw the ball down faster than he had ever done before. It bounced perfectly on the perfect pitch. I struck it back over his head. Perfectly. Over the tea tent it flew, over the road and into the cornfield. Six runs.

We'd won. The silence of the crowd exploded like a lemonade bottle when you take the top off. They cheered, they clapped, they even shook Mrs Reeve-Smith's hand.

I was slapped on the back and everyone from the other team shook my hand, even the headmaster. Only Rupert Reeve-Smith turned his back on me.

When we got home that night there was a letter waiting from my mum. Dad was home for a few days and she wanted me to come home now too. Mr Hitler was losing the war and there would be little chance of bombs dropping on our dusty old town.

Next morning I packed my small suitcase and left Rupert's old school uniform on the bed. I walked down to the car. Mrs Reeve-Smith and Rupert were waiting beside it. The boy stretched out his hand to me. I looked at it.

The words seemed to stick in his mouth like toffee. "Well played, Porter," he said and he hated to say it. "Come back and see us ... after the war."

"Which war?" I asked. "The war against Mr Hitler? Or the war between your sort and mine?"

Mrs Reeve-Smith spluttered. Rupert looked at his shoes.

I climbed into the car. I didn't turn round. But I looked in the car mirror as I was driven away to the railway station and saw Rupert standing in the drive, watching me leave. He looked miserable.

Dad was waiting for me at the station back home. "Have a good time, son?" he asked.

"Not complaining," I said.

"A Porter never complains," Dad said and he messed my hair.

"What about you, Dad? Did you kill many Germans?"

"I'm a cook in the army, son. I think I've killed more British soldiers than Germans," and he laughed. Then he frowned. "We had some German prisoners at our camp," he said. "They were good fellers really. Not at all evil. One thing I learned from this war. You never know who your friend is."

I thought of Rupert and his world. Another England. "And you never know who your enemy is, Dad. You never know."

War Game

Germany, March 1939

Just before World War 2

Chapter 1
A City in the North

Every evening, after school, we played football in the park. Sometimes we played on after dark by the light of the gas lamps in the street.

And, every evening, the girl used to come and watch us play. She stood shivering in her thin, grey coat – the coat with a yellow star sewn on. Helmut, the pork-butcher's son, always walked past her and sneered, "Jew".

The girl just grinned back at him, happy to be noticed. Her grin lit up the evening gloom.

Sometimes, when we were short of players we let her play and then she glowed with joy. "What's your name?" I asked her.

"Esther," she said.

"I'm Hans," I told her.

"I know."

"Esther, I want you to stand in the penalty area – you know where the penalty area is?"

"Yes, Hans."

"And just sort of … get in the way. If you get a chance then shoot at the goal. You know what the goal is?"

"Yes, Hans. The big iron frame."

I nodded.

"You don't play the offside rule?" she asked suddenly.

I blinked. She knew more about football than I thought. "No offside rule. It caused too many arguments," I told her. "Just stand there. Shoot if you get the chance. You won't beat Helmut."

"No, Hans," she said and trotted onto the pitch. She was wearing big, black boots that looked too large for her skinny legs. She would never beat Helmut. He was bigger than the rest of us – well fed by his pork-butcher father – and he didn't care who got hurt. When Helmut stood in front of any of us, we were almost scared to shoot past him. Esther had no chance.

One evening, just before the war started, we were all playing football in the park. Esther too. It was almost dark and the gas lamps glowed yellow and lit up the leaves of the trees on the street. The light made the trees look like great, green balloons. I ran with the ball from the centre line. There was only Helmut to beat. He loomed large as a tree in front of me.

"Shoot!" my team yelled.

"Shoot!" Esther called. She was standing just to one side of Helmut.

"What are you waiting for, Hans?" Helmut jeered and spread himself wide so he was blocking my way.

I didn't shoot. I passed across to Esther. She ran onto the ball with the goal open in front of her. She swung her big, black boot at the heavy, leather ball and hit it well. But there was no power in her skinny right leg and the ball just rolled slowly towards the goal-line.

Helmut turned and dived and collected it in his hands that were as fat as his father's hams. He bounced the ball on the soft grass and ran forwards. Esther stood in his way. He lowered his head like a charging bull and hit Esther,

shoulder to shoulder. It was a fair charge in the rules of the game.

Esther seemed to rise off the ground and fly through the air. Helmut booted the ball skywards but we weren't watching it. We'd all stopped and we looked towards Esther as she lay on the grass. She stirred. She sat up. She rose stiffly to her feet. "Good save, Helmut," she said. She looked across at me. "Sorry I missed, Hans. Good pass."

"It doesn't matter," I said. "Are you all right?"

Suddenly that grin lit up her face. "Great!" she laughed, but she was limping a little as she walked away. Helmut glared at her. "Jew," he snarled.

Chapter 2
War

War came. Not much changed at first.
We played at being German soldiers instead
of being German footballers. And we were
German airmen, spreading our arms and
roaring through the streets, shooting down
British planes. Helmut said he was a bomber
and his show of dropping bombs on London was
really rude – and funny.

The gas lights were turned off in the
evenings now and we hurried indoors to hear

the news on the radio. Of course we were winning the war. We always knew we would.

The iron goalposts were taken from the park one day. "Gone to be made into guns to shoot the British!" we joked as we saw them go.

Then the day came when our soldiers marched down our streets, dressed in their grey greatcoats and carrying their cold steel guns. We cheered, but we were frightened. We followed them down the wide road with its tall trees to the blocks of flats by the river. We stood at the corner and watched.

The soldiers crashed through the doors and came out herding everyone in front of them at gunpoint. Men, women, children, old and young. But every one wore the yellow star.

Helmut leaned towards me. "They're taking the Jews away."

"Where?"

"Don't know. But Herr Hitler doesn't want them in Germany. They're traitors, you know," Helmut said. "That means they're our enemies even though they live in our country."

That's when I saw Esther, her grey coat thinner than ever, her black hair flapping in the cold wind. A soldier was standing behind her with a gun. She must have been terrified. I was. But she reached up for her mother's hand, gave her bright smile and said something to comfort her.

Then she turned and smiled at the soldier with the gun. The soldier turned his face away.

I stepped forward. "Where are you going?" Helmut asked.

"To say goodbye to Esther!" I told him.

"Fool," he snarled and grabbed my arm in his ham-fist and pulled me back roughly. "You'll end up in the same place as her if you're not careful," he hissed and dragged me back towards our street.

"What place is that, Helmut?" I asked.

"Don't ask," he muttered.

But as the war went on we heard the stories. The Jews were taken to camps, they said. They were locked away and made to work for Germany. Some said they were killed. I didn't care that much. I was young. But some nights Esther's smile haunted my dreams.

Then the war started to go badly for us. They didn't say that on the radio of course, but we knew. Our fathers were taken off to fight for Herr Hitler's army in Russia. And the British started to bomb our city.

Every night we huddled in our cellars and felt the ground shake. In the mornings, we came out onto the street and saw our houses shattered and rubble spilling onto the roads.

The park grew wild and where we played football the grass was torn by the bombs. There was a hole where Helmut's goal used to be.

And it was hard to find food. Mothers waited for hours to get bread and when they brought it home it was dry and gritty. We made coffee from acorn powder and our soup was mainly water. Even Helmut got hardly any meat. We grew thin.

"We must join the Hitler Youth!" Helmut told us one day. "We are so close to winning this war. Herr Hitler needs our help."

Where Helmut led, we followed. In a week we were marching proudly around the streets in our new uniforms. We learned to fire a gun and how to swear like a soldier. But we knew that the real soldiers treated us as kids.

"We're losing the war," I said one day as we huddled in a cellar trying to shelter from the bombs.

"You could be shot for saying that," Helmut said.

"They are bombing us in the daytime now, Helmut," I told him. "Where are our fighter planes to stop them?"

"The German Army is fighting in Russia," he said grimly. "Winning the war."

"While we're being bombed?" I asked.

"What do a few bombs on a town matter?" he laughed, but he wouldn't look me in the eye when he said it.

Another explosion shook the cellar. Rubble showered down and blocked the door. We were choked by falling dust. It was night before they dug us out that time. A bright red night. Fires lit the docks, the railway yards and the factories. Flames reflected in Helmut's tear-filled eyes.

"We're losing the war, Helmut," I said softly.

"I will never lose. I do not like to lose. I would die rather than lose," he sniffed. I'd never seen Helmut cry before.

He'd never cried before the war when we were kids. Now he cried when we were fighters. War changes people.

Chapter 3
After the War

We heard the news on the radio. "Adolf Hitler is dead. Germany has surrendered. The British, the Americans, the Russians and the French armies will take charge of Germany."

"Please don't let it be the Russians who come here," my mother moaned.

At least the bombing stopped. We wandered onto the smashed streets, blinking at the light like bears waking up after their winter sleep.

We did not wear our uniforms. Some people hid them in the cellars. Some threw them in the river. We wore our old clothes. We'd grown taller but thinner and they fitted badly. We gathered on street corners looking like scarecrows.

Helmut's huge hands stuck out from the shrunken sleeves of his jacket – my bony knees showed through my frayed, black trousers. Each day someone new seemed to join us on the corner. Some were from the old gang who had played football in the park five years before. Some never showed up.

Then, one early May day, someone kicked a piece of rounded brick in the middle of the road. It flew in the air. Helmut stretched up a broad hand and caught it easily. Then he rolled it back down the street towards me. He took off his cap and snatched one off the head of another boy. He dropped a cap at either side of him and looked at me.

"There you are, Hans," he said. "A goal. Just like the old days. See if you can beat me!"

I shrugged and kicked the brick. I hit it well with the toe-cap of my boot and it flew towards the goal. Someone cheered, "Goal!" but Helmut reached up lazily and caught it in the air. He was as brilliant as ever.

"Let's play in the park," a small boy called Carl said.

"We haven't got two teams," I said. Just enough for one team. Eleven of us.

"Five a side," Helmut said.

We ran across to the park. It took us all morning to clear the grass of the stone and broken brick and concrete. We filled the holes with the rubble. By noon we were ready to play. "I've got a ball I made out of rags in my house," Carl told us. "Meet here after lunch and we'll have a game."

Chapter 4
The Goal

Eleven of us lined up. "Hans and I will pick the teams," Helmut said. No one argued. We threw a coin to decide who chose first. Helmut won. He was able to pick a team of six while I was left with five.

"I never lose," he said.

"I know," I said with a sigh.

I turned to sort out my team and looked around the park. The trees were broken and black, yet new shoots and buds were growing from the stumps. There were two tall trees that used to stand by the gates – before they took the railings away to melt them down for tanks. That's where I saw her. She was standing between the two bomb-blasted trees.

Esther.

She was a little taller but even thinner. Her eyes were darker as if they had looked on death. We all had. But at that time I had no idea just how much death she had seen in the camps. Far more than the rest of us put together.

Her coat was a new, black woollen one – and there was no yellow star on it. Her skinny legs were wrapped in black stockings and her boots were shining black. In her arms she carried a football.

The boys turned and looked at her silently. She crossed the rubble slowly, shyly. She held out the ball. "The Americans gave me this when they let us out of the camps," she said. "Can we use it?"

We nodded. We couldn't find any words to speak to her. At last I was able to turn and say to Helmut, "You have six players. Esther will have to be on my side."

She smiled. Helmut nodded. For the second and last time in my life I saw tears in his eyes. I looked at my watch – it hadn't worked since 1941 but I still wore it and pretended. "Twenty minutes each way!" I shouted. I put my fingers to my lips and whistled.

For the next half hour that park rang with something it hadn't heard in five years. Laughter.

Esther was as useless as ever. She jumped up and down on the place where the penalty spot should have been. She yelled at us – but she didn't *do* anything useful.

It was hard to play on rubble. The ball bounced and bumped everywhere. But, for that half hour we forgot the dark past and the bleak future. We were children again. Then it happened. Just as it had happened all those years before.

I ran with the ball from the centre line. There was only Helmut to beat. He loomed large as a tree in front of me.

"Shoot!" my team screamed.

"Shoot!" Esther called. She was standing just to one side of Helmut.

"What are you waiting for, Hans?" Helmut jeered and spread himself wide so he was blocking my way.

I didn't shoot. I passed sideways to Esther. She ran onto the ball with the goal open in front of her. She swung her big, black boot at the heavy, leather ball and hit it well. But there was no power in her skinny right leg and the ball just rolled slowly towards the goal-line.

Helmut dived.

Maybe the ball struck a piece of broken brick. Maybe Helmut slipped. Maybe he was blinded by tears. Or maybe he missed the ball because he wanted to. All these years later he still won't tell me how he missed it.

But Helmut missed it.

The ball rolled over the line.

There was silence for five long seconds then little Carl cheered. "Goal! Esther scored!"

"Goal!" our team cheered.

"I scored a goal?" Esther gasped. And then all the boys were up around her, hugging her and shouting.

I looked at my broken watch. "Full time," I called. "We won. One-nil! We won one-nil!"

Everyone turned to Helmut. He would not be pleased. He picked up the ball and walked slowly to the group around Esther. His face was grim. Everyone but Esther seemed to shrink back.

"I scored a goal!" Esther breathed. That grin lit up the grim, grey park as it had done when she last played there. As it had done when Helmut charged her to the ground.

Now he placed the ball under his long left arm. He stretched out his right hand. "Great goal, Esther," he said.

"I scored," she said. Slowly she raised her hand to shake his. Her little hand vanished in his huge paw.

"Well done," he said. He pulled her towards him and wrapped an arm around her shoulder.

He walked out of the park with that arm still around her shoulder.

Ten boys stared after them as if we had seen a miracle.

Perhaps we had.

Our books are tested
for children and young people by
children and young people.

Thanks to everyone who consulted on
a manuscript for their time and effort in
helping us to make our books better
for our readers.